Haunted Holidays

VALENTERROR

Fountaindale Public Library
Bolingbrook, IL
(630) 759-2102

by Linda Joy Singleton
illustrated by George Ermos

Spellbound

An Imprint of Magic Wagon
abdobooks.com

FOR BREONNA, MY ALMOST-VALENTINE-BIRTHDAY
GIRL WHO LOVES BOOKS. -LJS

abdobooks.com

Published by Magic Wagon, a division of ABDO, PO Box 398166,
Minneapolis, Minnesota 55439. Copyright © 2020 by Abdo Consulting
Group, Inc. International copyrights reserved in all countries. No part of this
book may be reproduced in any form without written permission from the
publisher. Spellbound™ is a trademark and logo of Magic Wagon.
Printed in the United States of America, North Mankato, Minnesota.

092019
012020

**THIS BOOK CONTAINS
RECYCLED MATERIALS**

Written by Linda Joy Singleton
Illustrated by George Ermos
Edited by Bridget O'Brien
Design Contributors: Christina Doffing & Victoria Bates

Library of Congress Control Number: 2019942012

Publisher's Cataloging-in-Publication Data

Names: Singleton, Linda Joy, author. | Ermos, George, illustrator.
Title: Valenterror / by Linda Joy Singleton ; illustrated by George Ermos.
Description: Minneapolis, Minnesota : Magic Wagon, 2020. | Series:
    Haunted holidays
Summary: Devin resents his substitute teacher and decides to create a
    wicked Valentine's Day card for her, but instead of scaring his teacher,
    the monstrous card turns on him.
Identifiers: ISBN 9781532136641 (lib. bdg.) | ISBN 9781532137242
    (ebook) | ISBN 9781532137549 (Read-to-Me ebook)
Subjects: LCSH: Valentine's Day--Juvenile fiction. | Teachers--Juvenile
    fiction. | Anger--Juvenile fiction. | Greeting cards--Juvenile fiction. |
    Monsters--Juvenile fiction. | Holidays--Juvenile fiction.
Classification: DDC (Fic)--dc23

TABLE OF CONTENTS

Chapter One
THE SUBSTITUTE

Devin glared at the substitute teacher. His real teacher, Miss Hart, was nice and made learning fun. But the **SUBSTITUTE**, Mrs. Rupp, was totally unfair!

"I don't want to make sappy **valentines**," Devin told his friend Jack.

"Why not?" Jack CUT a heart shape out of blue paper.

5

"Mom already bought a box of **valentines**. There's even a valentine for the teacher. But that's for Miss Hart when she comes back from her vacation."

"Teacher's pet," Jack **TEASED**.

"Am not!" Devin glared. "Take it back or I'll make you eat that paper."

Jack just LAUGHED. "If you don't want to make a **valentine**, tell Mrs. Rupp you won't do it. I dare you."

Devin looked at the **SUBSTITUTE** teacher. She sat at Miss Hart's desk, in Miss Hart's chair, writing with Miss Hart's pens.

He turned to Jack with a wicked grin.

"Mrs. Rupp wants a valentine so I'll give her one," he said. "But my valentine won't be sweet. It will be scary. Valentine BEWARE!"

Chapter Two
BEWARE VALENTINE

Devin frowned at his craft paper.

Green, blue, and yellow were too nice.

He wanted SCARY paper.

"Here," a voice said from behind

him. "Would you like to use my

SPECIAL paper?"

Devin turned around to face the new girl Yuliya. She lived in the WEIRD Wildmare Mansion (nicknamed Nightmare Mansion). No one was **brave** enough to be her friend.

But Devin was feeling **brave** today, so he took the paper. It was the strangest paper he'd ever seen.

Black claw marks scraped down the bone-white paper like *WILD* animal SCRATCHES. Bright red blobs splattered like blood drops. There were even matching red envelopes.

"COOL!" Devin said. "Where'd you get it?"

"I found it." She leaned in to whisper. "In my attic."

Devin shivered. "Weren't you

SCARED to go there?"

"Nothing **SCARES** me."

"Nothing scares me either," he

bragged.

"We'll see," she said with a

MYSTERIOUS smile.

Devin shrugged. Yuliya was as

WEIRD as her freaky house.

But her paper was PERFECT

for his plan.

17

He drew a picture of Mrs. Rupp. He gave her sharp fangs, a **HUGE** spider body, six hairy legs, and slimy red eyeballs. Gross warts covered her monstrous face, and a lizard tongue whipped out like a rope.

Devin didn't write: "Be mine, Valentine."

Instead he wrote, "Don't be mine, Valentine. BEWARE!"

He hid the **valentine** in his backpack.

At lunch break, he *snuck* into the classroom and left the valentine on Mrs. Rupp's desk. He was turning to leave when he heard . . .

PLOPP! CRACKLE!
GRRRR!

He whirled around and *GASPED*.

A dark baseball-sized blob FLOATED over the teacher's desk. It swirled, SQUAWKED, and grew bigger than a basketball. Fuzzy floppy legs popped out—SIX of them! A long green tongue snaked from the swirling blob, and bloody slime eyes blazed evil in a warty face.

"My valentine!" Devin shrieked. "It's alive!"

Chapter Three
PAPER PREDATOR

Devin raced for the door. But the slick green tongue **SLITHERED** ahead of him. It wrapped around the doorknob like a snake.

"Let me out!" Devin **banged** against the door.

The spiderlike blob hissed,

"BEWARE, VALENTINE!"

"I am not your valentine!" Devin SHOUTED.

He stared in horror as the monster grew larger than Miss Hart's desk. Sharp fangs oozed with slime as creepy legs crawled closer.

"Be mine, be mine, **Valentine**," the monster chanted. "Be mine."

"Go away!" Devin ducked behind a desk and hid.

But a long leg found Devin and grabbed his ankle. It wrapped Devin in a **DEATH** grip and dragged him across the floor—toward the oozing sharp fangs!

"**HELP**!" Devin trembled. "Don't hurt me!"

"Be mine, yummy **valentine**!" Snorts and slobbering sounds bubbled from the monster, and the fangs drew open wider.

Devin fought back, hitting, kicking and squirming, but he couldn't break free. He was being pulled past chairs and desks, headed right for the monster's *DEADLY* mouth!

31

"Be mine, be mine, valentine,"

the monster chanted. "Beware!"

"HELP! Someone help!"

Devin hollered.

He grabbed onto his own desk, but
the monster was stronger. His hands
slipped. Devin **STRUGGLED**
but he couldn't hold on. He was going
to be a monster snack.

Chapter Four
MONSTER SLAYER

As Devin was dragged past Jack's spot, he remembered that **sloppy** Jack never put anything away.

He lunged toward Jack's desk and grabbed the scissors. He reached down, aimed the scissors, and sliced the slimy leg that held his ankle.

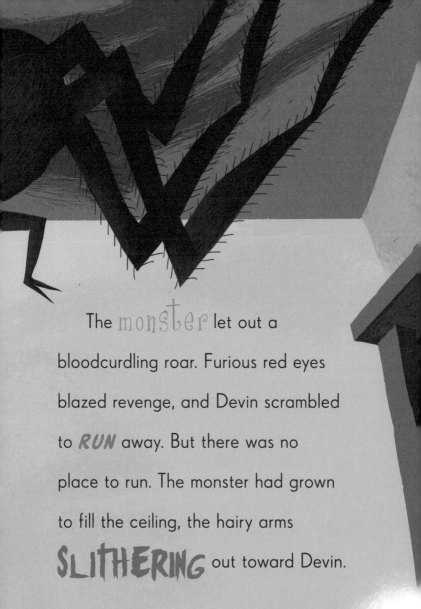

The monster let out a
bloodcurdling roar. Furious red eyes
blazed revenge, and Devin scrambled
to **RUN** away. But there was no
place to run. The monster had grown
to fill the ceiling, the hairy arms
SLITHERING out toward Devin.

"Be mine, be mine, **Valentine**," the mᴏɴsᴛᴇʀ's fanged mouth chanted.

"No!" Devin sʜᴏᴜᴛᴇᴅ, wishing he'd never created the ugly monster. "I made you and I can **DESTROY** you!"

Instead of going to the door and trying to force it open, in a *WILD* panic Devin bolted for the teacher's desk. Jumping over and jogging around **DEADLY** spider legs, Devin lunged for the desktop. He grabbed the unusual valentine.

Before the monster could stop him, Devin **RIPPED** the paper into tiny pieces.

Poof! **Swish!** **Whoosh!**

The spider-monster vanished.

Devin dumped the torn

valentine into the garbage—

where it belonged.

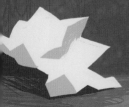

A short time later, Mrs. Rupp returned to the room. Everything was back to *NORMAL*, except Devin. He was covered in SWEAT and his heart still **POUNDED**.

He'd never been so relieved to

see a teacher in his life—even a

SUBSTITUTE!

Mrs. Rupp was definitely better

than the six-legged, slimy-fanged

monster.

When Devin's classmates returned

from lunch, Mrs. Rupp handed out

valentines for each student.

She **STOPPED** at Devin's desk last.

"I made a **special valentine** for you," she said

with an odd gleam in her eyes.